For my family, with you I am always home.

The book you are about to read
is no ordinary book.

This is the story about a very
special family.

A family who share a glimpse
into their world.

A story through which they
share some of their favourite
things.

What is your Favourite sound, one that brings a memory of warmth and joy?

The rhythmic claps of Akara.*

Clap! clap!clap!

Girls in a line.

Symphony of coordination,

One, two, three your turn!

Swoosh!!
The sleigh going down,
faster, faster!
Eyes wide-open,
Pure delight.

Pling! Pling!
My turn! My turn to press!
I love the bell on the bus.

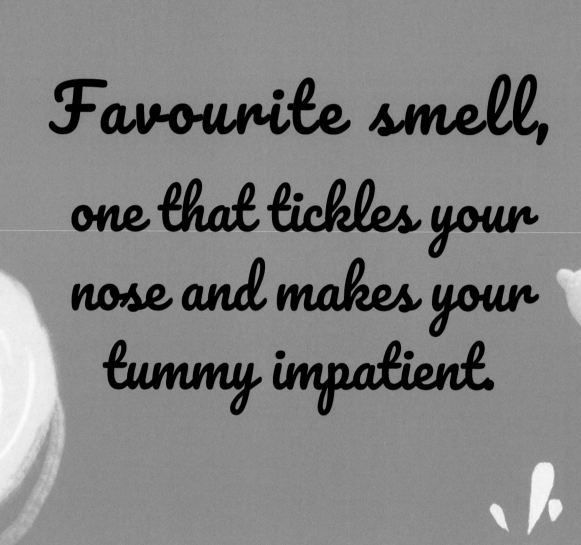

Favourite smell,
one that tickles your
nose and makes your
tummy impatient.

The mouth-watering seafood delight of Ebbeh. Crabs, shrimp, cassava, lots of lime and chilli.

Freshly baked Gingerbread cookies.
Truly the sweetest scent ever!

Favourite Taste,

a delicious little something that leaves you wanting more.

The iconic fish Benechin with
tamarind and fresh lime,
all day for me.

Peanut butter Domoda with hot steaming rice. Always the best to warm me up inside.

I want meatballs and potatoes,
just like Alfons!*

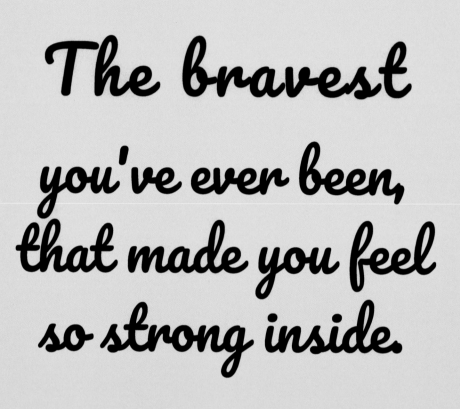

The bravest
you've ever been,
that made you feel
so strong inside.

Stroking a crocodile at katchikali pond.

Riding a roller coaster
at Gröna Lund!

I climbed to the tippy-top of the slide!

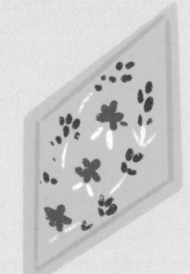

Favourite pastime,
that always brings smile.

Sitting with my family, warm and cosy on a winter afternoon.

Flying kites made with sticks and glue with grandpa.

Digging in the sandbox with
Nirupama and Mama.

Favourite place
you've ever been,
that fills your heart with a
sense of peace.

Makasutu, surrounded by nature,
floating quietly on a river boat.

Chasing 'sky fans' in Gotland
as they spin silently.

In your arms,
that's the best place
we will ever be.

The Gambia and Sweden are the places this family call home. In this book, they shared some of their favourites for you to discover.

The Gambia

Akara - A game played by schools children in The Gambia which involves clapping and stomping to a rhythm.

Ebbeh- A cassava and palm oil dish, with an assortment of seafood. Often served with lots of pepper and lime

Benechin- Also known as Jollof rice. A one pot dish eaten all over West Africa. Often served with fish or meat and an assortment of vegetables.

Domoda- A west African peanut butter stew served with rice and vegetables.

Katchikally - A crocodile pond in The Gambia.

Makasutu - An ecotourism woodland reserve in The Gambia.

Swedish Meatballs - A traditional dish with soft meatballs, served with gravy, boiled potatoes, lingonberry jam, and pickled cucumber.

Gotland- The largest island in Sweden, rich in natural beauty and cultural history.

Gröna Lund- The largest amusement park in the Swedish capital of Stockholm.

Swedish Gingerbread cookies- Often home-baked thin biscuits that are decorated with glaze and candy.

Alfons Åberg/Alfie Atkins- a much loved fictional character.

Sweden

Emily Joof is a multicultural story teller based in Sweden, with an encompassing love for sunflowers. Her stories center on the Afrodiasporan experience, bringing cultural diversity to the fore.

Emily is published under Mbife Books where all her writing is featured.
Find out more at www.mbife.com

Sawyer Cloud is a self-taught illustrator and author of children's books living in Madagascar. She loves telling stories with her illustrations, using warm colours and diverse characters.

Sawyer is now represented by one of the biggest agencies in the world, Advocate Art agency.
Find out more at https://sawyer.cloud.html

More Books from Mbife Books:

Mangoes & Monkeybread;
Fruity Fun with Ella & Louis

Available on Amazon
in English, French, Swedish and Wolof.

If you enjoyed the book, do leave a review on Amazon!

We would love to hear from you. Get in touch with us and tell us about your home on www.mbife.com or on social media. .

Instagram: @mbife_Books
Twitter: @mbifebooks
Facebook: MbifeBooks

Tag us! #OurFavouritethings #mbifebooks